For children
of all ages with
Wisdom,
Clear Sight,
Equality,
Generosity, and
Right Judgment.

Margaret K. McElderry Books
An imprint of Simon & Schuster
Children's Publishing Division
1230 Avenue of the Americas,
New York, New York 10020
Copyright © 2008 by Demi
Book design by Michael Nelson
The text for this book is set in Caxton.
The illustrations for this book are rendered in paint and ink with Chinese silk brocade.
Title calligraphy by Jeanyee Wong
Manufactured in China
10 9 8 7 6 5 4 3 2 1
LIBRARY OF CONGRESS CATALOGING-IN-PUBLICATION DATA
Demi. • The girl who drew a phoenix / Demi.—1st ed. • p. cm.
    Summary: A young girl acquires the qualities of the miraculous phoenix—
    wisdom, clear sight, equality, generosity, and right judgment—
    by practicing drawing the mythical bird.
    ISBN-13: 978-1-4169-5347-0 (hardcover)
    ISBN-10: 1-4169-5347-7 (hardcover)
    [1. Phoenix (Mythical bird)—Fiction.
    2. Drawing—Fiction. 3. China—Fiction.] I. Title.
    PZ7.D3925Gi 2008
    [E]—dc22 • 2007015411

FIRST
EDITION

THE GIRL WHO DREW A Phoenix

Demi

MARGARET K. McELDERRY BOOKS

New York London Toronto Sydney

Up in the heavens the phoenix were flying.
They lit up the sun and the stars and the skies
with the lights from their sparkling tails,
and they nourished all the heavens!

As the Supreme Female Powers and Principles of the universe, the phoenix saw that all life was born and maintained in heaven and on earth. They helped others wherever they could— making the universe one integral whole.

The heavens were also filled with little phoenix, learning all the phoenix powers of Wisdom, Clear Sight, Equality, Generosity, and Right Judgment. They learned about the heavens, and they learned about the earth, too.

On earth there was a little girl named Feng Huang. One day she found a feather of a phoenix. What a treasure! She had never seen a real phoenix before, but she knew about their marvelous powers and wanted them. Maybe by drawing a phoenix, she thought, she would get some.

And so Feng Huang made a rough outline of the bird on her garden wall. Some of her friends came by and looked at the drawing.

One friend said, "It looks more like an owl than a phoenix!"

Another said, "It reminds me of a hawk!"

Still another said, "I think it's a bat!"

Everyone laughed at the ugliness of the bird and the clumsiness of the artist.

The Queen Phoenix, who was sitting on a star,
looked down from her heavenly perch
and saw that Feng Huang needed help.

With a flourish of sparkles and stars, she swooped down to earth and gracefully landed before Feng Huang, who was totally astonished!

Then Feng Huang practiced drawing phoenixes everywhere!
But the spirit of the phoenix did not come through.

The Queen Phoenix said, "I will stay with you all day so you can practice drawing me. After that you must continue to practice very hard on your own."

The Queen Phoenix decided Feng Huang must
know the powers of the phoenix to truly draw
them, and so she returned to Feng Huang with
a list.

"Follow this list!" she said, and disappeared
again with a flourish of sparkles and stars!

Full of wonder, Feng Huang stared at the list:

Find the Phoenix of Wisdom.

Feng Huang looked far and wide, but without any luck. So she sat down and deeply thought of the Phoenix of Wisdom.

Suddenly in a burst of flames the Phoenix of Wisdom appeared.

The Phoenix said, "To have Wisdom you must pass through the fire of Ignorance! Draw away all Ignorance!"

Feng Huang drew and drew away all Ignorance, and suddenly felt herself drawing Wisdom. She felt completely changed! She thanked the Phoenix very much and looked at her list:

Find the Phoenix of Clear Sight.

Feng Huang sat down and deeply thought of the Phoenix of Clear Sight. Suddenly in a burst of flames the Phoenix of Clear Sight appeared.

The Phoenix said, "To have Clear Sight
you must pass through the fire of Anger!
Draw away all Anger!"

Feng Huang drew and drew away all Anger,
and suddenly felt herself drawing Clear Sight.
She felt completely changed! She thanked the Phoenix
very much and looked at her list:

Find the Phoenix of Equality.

Feng Huang sat down and deeply thought of the Phoenix of Equality. Suddenly in a burst of flames the Phoenix of Equality appeared.

The Phoenix said, "To have Equality you must pass through the fire of Selfishness! Draw away all Selfishness!"

Feng Huang drew and drew away all Selfishness, and suddenly she felt herself drawing Equality. She felt completely changed! She thanked the Phoenix very much and looked at her list:

Find the Phoenix of Generosity.

Feng Huang sat down and deeply thought
of the Phoenix of Generosity. Suddenly in
a burst of flames the Phoenix of
Generosity appeared.

The Phoenix said, "To have
Generosity you must pass through the fire of
Greed! Draw away all Greed!"

Feng Huang drew and drew away all Greed,
and suddenly she felt herself drawing
Generosity. She felt completely changed!
She thanked the Phoenix very much
and looked at the last item on her list:

Find the Phoenix of Right Judgment.

Feng Huang sat down and deeply thought of the Phoenix of Right Judgment. Suddenly in a burst of flames the Phoenix of Right Judgment appeared.

The Phoenix said, "To have Right Judgment you must pass through the fire of Jealousy! Draw away all Jealousy!"

Feng Huang drew and drew away all Jealousy, and suddenly she felt herself drawing Right Judgment. She felt completely changed! She thanked the Phoenix very much and went home.

Feng Huang began drawing, and soon a glorious phoenix appeared with a crown like sapphires, wings like rubies, and feathers like diamonds!

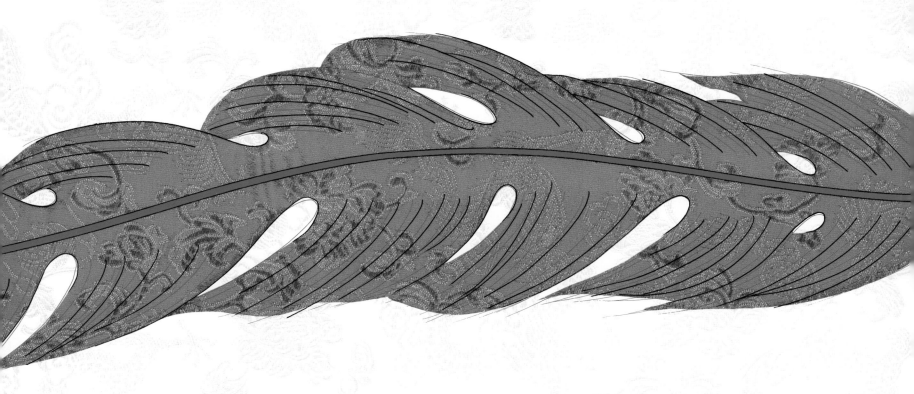

When Feng Huang's friends gathered around this time, they were all completely amazed!
Those who had teased her before were stunned by the wonderful skill of the artist!

Feng Huang had learned so many powers of the
phoenix that with her last touch—dotting the eye—
her phoenix soared high up into the sky, where it flew
for three days and nights!

With a flourish of sparkles and stars, Feng Huang's glorious phoenix returned to earth. Feng Huang wanted to share her new powers with all her friends, and so she invited them to ride on her phoenix through the heavens.

As they flew past the stars and comets,
the phoenix taught them:

*In the multitude of words
there certainly are mistakes.*

*It is difficult to get a good word;
it is easy to give a bad one.*

*And much mischief comes
from opening the mouth!*

She also taught them the powers of
Wisdom,
Clear Sight,
Equality,
Generosity, and
Right Judgment.
So then when they drew, the spirit of the
phoenix really did come through.